THIS **ELEPHANT & PIGGIE** BOOK
BELONGS TO:

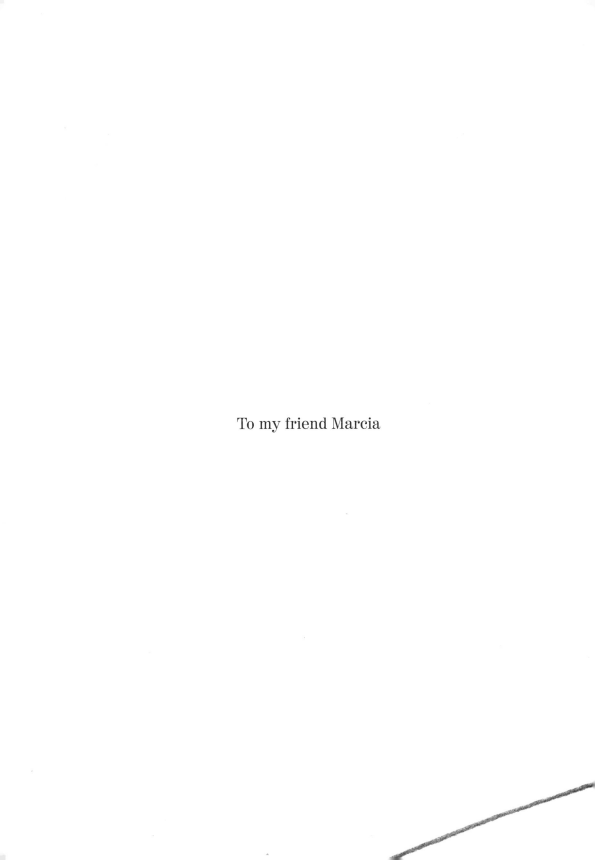

To my friend Marcia

# My Friend Is Sad

By Mo Willems

WALKER BOOKS
AND SUBSIDIARIES
LONDON · BOSTON · SYDNEY · AUCKLAND

An **ELEPHANT & PIGGIE** Book

4

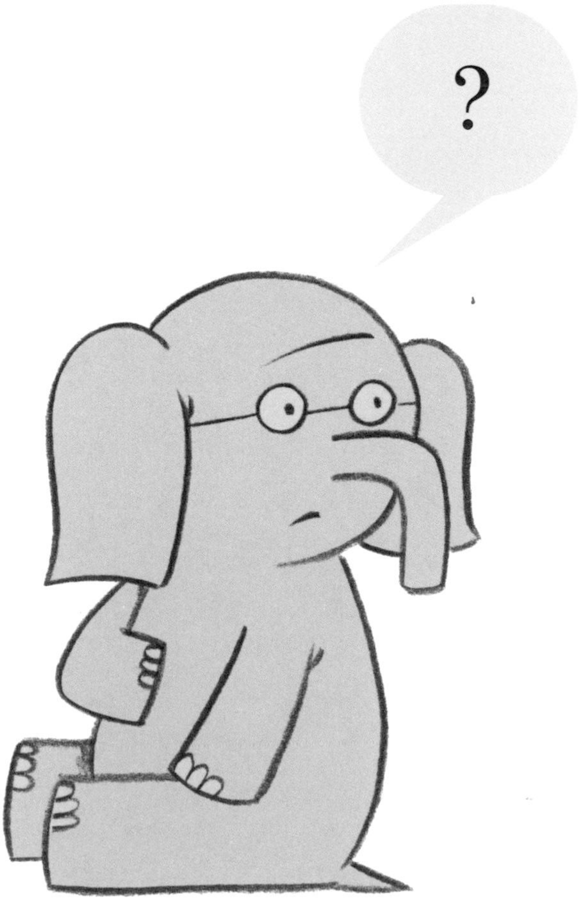

9

Ohhh…

Gerald loves cowboys.
But he is still sad.

13

Ohhh…

Clowns are funny.
But he is still sad.

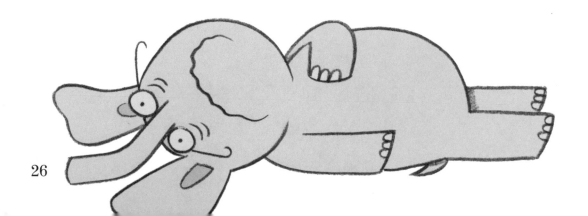

I am sorry. I wanted to make you happy. But you are still sad.

I am happy because you are here!

But I was so sad, Piggie.
So very SAD!

39

Then I saw a clown!

41

43

THERE
WAS
MORE!

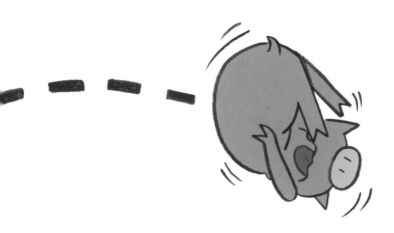

# A COOL, COOL ROBOT!

And my best friend
was not there
to see it with me.

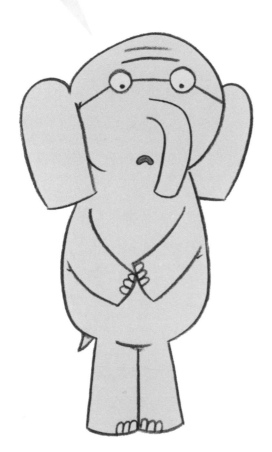

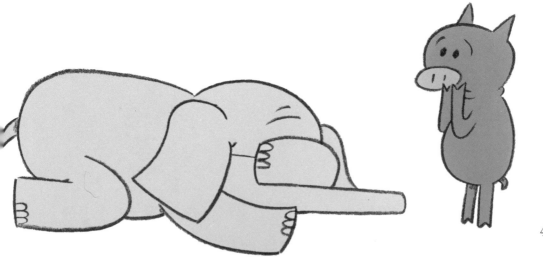

49

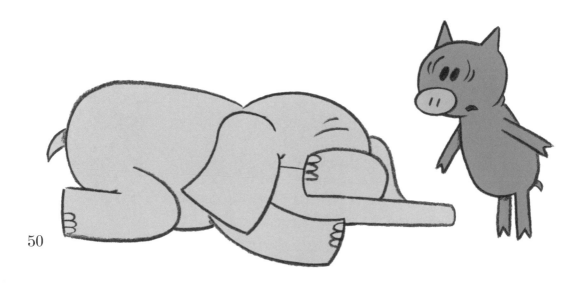

50

I am here NOW!

You are!
You are here now!

# My friend is here now!

56